Sp

Please return/renew this item by the last date shown

**Herefordshire
Libraries**

*Herefordshire
Council*

Do dh'Eleanor agus Mìcheal
J.D.

To my spider-loving sisters,
Lyn and Angela
L.P.

EGMONT
We bring stories to life

Book Band: Purple

First published in Great Britain 2002 by Egmont UK Limited
The Yellow Building, 1 Nicholas Road, London W11 4AN
Text copyright © Julia Donaldson 2002
Illustrations copyright © Liz Pichon 2002
The author and illustrator have asserted their moral rights.
ISBN 978 1 4052 0072 1
20 19 18 17 16 15 14
A CIP catalogue record for this title is available from the British Library
Printed in Singapore
40668/18

EGMONT LUCKY COIN

Our story began over a century ago, when seventeen-year-old Egmont Harald Petersen found a coin in the street.

He was on his way to buy a flyswatter, a small hand-operated printing machine that he then set up in his tiny apartment.

The coin brought him such good luck that today Egmont has offices in over 30 countries around the world. And that lucky coin is still kept at the company's head offices in Denmark.

Spinderella

Julia Donaldson

Illustrated by Liz Pichon

Blue Bananas

The children of Scuttleton Primary School were eating their dinner – fish fingers, potatoes and peas. High up above them, on the ceiling of the dinner hall, the spiders of Scuttleton Primary School were eating their dinner – flies, flies and flies.

Delicious!

'How many flies have we got today, Mum?'

asked Spinderella, the smallest spider.

'Lots,' said Mum.

'Loads,' said her nine brothers and sisters,

with their mouths full.

'Loads isn't a number,' complained

Spinderella.

'Never mind about numbers. Eat up

your flies,' said her mum.

After dinner, the children went out

to play. Spinderella swung down

from the web like a yo-yo. She hung

there looking out of the window

into the playground.

'It's football!' she cried.

In a flash her mum and her nine brothers and sisters were swinging beside her. All the spiders' eyes were fixed on the football game.

'What a tackle!' they cried, and,

'Go, go, go!'

Yippee!

Then, 'GOAL!' they all yelled. They clapped
their spindly legs and nearly let go of their
threads. The children scored goal after goal.

'How many goals is that, Mum?' asked
Spinderella.

'Lots,' said Mum.

'Loads,' said her nine brothers and sisters.

'What a family!' Spinderella sighed. 'How
will I *ever* learn about numbers?'

When all the children had gone home, Spinderella said, 'Why don't *we* play football?'

'Don't be silly, we haven't got a ball,' said one of her brothers.

'I can see a little pea on the floor,' said Spinderella. 'We can use that.'

Perfect!

Mum was the ref with a whistle made from a broken drinking straw. She chose Speedy and Scrabble as the captains of each team.

Speedy was the fastest runner, so nearly
all the other spiders decided to join his
team. That team scored all the goals.

14

'It's not fair!' the spiders on Scrabble's team started shouting.

'Yes it is! You're just jealous!' shouted the spiders on Speedy's team.

To make things worse, the spiders hurt their legs kicking the pea!

Before long they were all quarrelling,
moaning, and kicking each other instead
of the pea. Mum had to blow her whistle.

'How many should we have in each

team, Mum?' asked Spinderella.

'Er . . . lots,' said Mum.

'Loads,' said her nine brothers and sisters.

'I think both teams should have the same number,' said Spinderella.

'Shut up about numbers!' shouted the others.

'I'm only trying to help,' said Spinderella. But the others all turned on her. 'Down with numbers!' they yelled.

That night Spinderella felt too sad to sleep.

When morning came, she was still awake.

'I *wish* I could learn about numbers!'

she sighed.

'And so you shall!' came a loud voice.

Spinderella looked up and saw an

enormous hairy spider.

'Who are you?' asked Spinderella, amazed.

'I am your Hairy Godmother,' said the

enormous spider. 'Follow me!'

The Hairy Godmother scuttled off down a wall. Spinderella ran after her. 'Where are we going?' she asked. 'In here,' said the Hairy Godmother.

She ran into a classroom and up to the ceiling.

Below them were lots of children.

'Now, keep your eyes and ears open!'

she told Spinderella, and in a flash

she was gone.

A teacher came in with a
pile of football shirts.

'I want you to count yourselves,'
he said to the children. 'There should
be twenty of you, but let's check.'

At last!

Then came the most wonderful sound.
The children took turns to shout a
number, from one to twenty. Spinderella
swung joyfully backwards and forwards
in time to the counting.

The teacher gave
out the shirts.
'Put them on
and find the
other children
with the same
colour shirt,'
he said.
Soon there were
two groups
of children.
'How many
in each team?'
asked the teacher.

1
2
3
4
5
6
7
8
9
10

I knew it!

The children
counted again.
'Ten reds,' said
a girl in red.
'Ten blues,' said
a boy in blue.
'The same
number!'
shouted
Spinderella.

27

She was so excited that she let go of her thread, just as the school clock struck twelve.

'Look! A spider! Squash it!' screamed someone. Spinderella froze in terror.

'Let's put it out of the window,' said

the teacher.

Suddenly Spinderella was outside.

'Help!' she called out, and 'Mum!'

but no one answered her.

 Two tears trickled out of

Spinderella's eyes. 'I'm lost!'

she wailed. 'I'll never see my

mum again.'

But then she looked around her.
She could see two football goals. 'It's
the playground!' she said to herself.

'The dinner hall can't be far away.'

 Spinderella scuttled round

the outside of the school,

looking in all the windows.

At last she came to the dinner hall.

The window was open. Spinderella ran

inside. She rushed into the web, panting.

'I can count up to twenty!' she cried.

'Never mind about that. Eat up

your flies,' said Mum.

'I'm going to count them first,' said Spinderella, and she did. 'I've got fourteen flies!' she told her brothers and sisters. 'So what?' they said.

Fourteen juicy flies!

'Numbers are boring. Down with numbers! Up with flies and football!'

Who cares?

That night the spiders decided to have another football game. But once again it was a disaster, and Mum had to keep blowing her whistle.

'Mum,' said Spinderella. 'I've been counting, and there are ten of us. I think we need five spiders on each side.'

Five a side!

Some of the spiders muttered, 'Down with numbers!' but Mum shut them up. Spinderella sorted them into two teams of five.

Pheeeeeeeeep!

Then Mum blew her whistle for the new game to start.

This time everything was different. No one quarrelled or kicked each other.

Spinderella was in Scrabble's team, and she also helped Mum keep score.

Well done, Mum!

At half time, both teams had scored

three goals. 'Three all,' said Mum.

But still the spiders kept hurting their

spindly legs kicking the pea.

'Ow!' they said, and, 'We can't go on.'

'I *wish* we had some football boots!'

sighed Spinderella.

'And so you shall!' came a voice from behind her. It was the Hairy Godmother again!

You're back!

'How many boots do you each need?' asked the Hairy Godmother.

'Lots,' said Mum.

'Loads,' said Spinderella's brothers and sisters.

'That's not good enough,' said the Hairy Godmother. 'I need to have a *number*.'

'Eight!' shouted Spinderella. 'We've each got eight legs, so we each need eight boots.'

'Done!' said the Hairy Godmother.

She clapped her legs.

There was a flash.

Eight!

Well done, Spinderella!

And there on the floor of the dinner hall were ten little piles of boots. Each pile had eight boots in it. The spiders put them on and laced them up.

Then they had a wonderful second half. They scored goal after goal. The Hairy Godmother clapped and clapped.

With only a minute left to go, the score was very close, Speedy's team had eight goals, and Scrabble's team had seven. Then Scrabble scored a goal.

'It's eight all!' muttered Spinderella. 'It's going to be a draw.'

But just then the ball came her way and she gave it an almighty kick. It shot straight into the goal, just a second before her mum blew the whistle.

Spinderella had scored the winning goal!

All the spiders ran up to her. They picked

her up and cheered. 'Up with Spinderella!'

they cried. 'Up with numbers!'

Spider's Legs!

A game for two people!

Are you my friend?

Yes!

To play Spider's Legs you first need to find a friend to play it with.

Next you need to find:

1 potato each for your spider's body.

2 raisins each for your spider's eyes.

8 drinking straws each. These will make your spider's legs.

You also need 1 dice, 1 felt-tip pen and 1 pencil.

In Spider's Legs you make you own spider and play the game at the same time! Whoever makes their spider first is the winner!

Follow the instructions carefully and ask a grown-up for help with the tricky bits.

He's a giant!

This is how your spider will look at the end.

Before you begin the game you both need to prepare your potato. Here is what you must do:

(1) Use the tip of a pencil to make two holes at the front of your potato. These holes are for your spider's eyes.

Ask a grown-up for help!

(2) With a felt-tip pen draw on a smiley mouth.

(3) Then use the pencil to make **four** holes on **each** side of your potato. These holes are for your spider's legs.

Ask a grown-up for help!

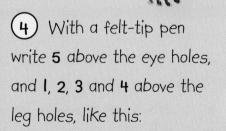

(4) With a felt-tip pen write **5** above the eye holes, and **1, 2, 3** and **4** above the leg holes, like this:

Now you are ready to start the game!

The Rules

Follow them carefully!

1 First, each player must roll the dice once.

What number did you roll?

What number did you get? Whoever gets the biggest number starts the game! Then you take turns.

2 When it's your turn, roll the dice.

Roll 1   Put straws in the holes you labelled **1**

Roll 2   Put straws in the holes you labelled **2**

Roll 3   Put straws in the holes you labelled **3**

Roll 4   Put straws in the holes you labelled **4**

Roll 5   Put the raisins in the holes you labelled **5**

You rolled a two!

Yippee! My spider gets two of his legs.

Watch out! If you roll a **6**, you must take away two of Spider's legs. Poor Spider!

Gulp!

But don't worry, on your next turn Spider can have his legs back again!